Words to Know Before You Read

defender

defensive

goalie

midfielders

opponents

opposition

organized

tenacious

terrapin

tortoise

www.rourkeeducationalmedia.com

Edited by Precious McKenzie
Illustrated by Anita DuFalla
Art Direction and Page Layout by Renee Brady

Library of Congress PCN Data

Team Captain / J. Jean Robertson
ISBN 978-1-61810-181-5 (hard cover) (alk. paper)
ISBN 978-1-61810-314-7 (soft cover)
Library of Congress Control Number: 2012936782

Rourke Educational Media
Printed in the United States of America,
North Mankato, Minnesota

Rourke
Educational Media
rourkeeducationalmedia.com

customerservice@rourkeeducationalmedia.com • PO Box 643328 Vero Beach, Florida 32964

TEAM CAPTAIN

By J. Jean Robertson
Illustrated by Anita DuFalla

Thank you fellow soccer players
for choosing me, Tallulah Turtle,
as your team captain.

You have all heard about my Uncle Toby of the Tidewater Terrapins. He played in the Terrific Turtle League.

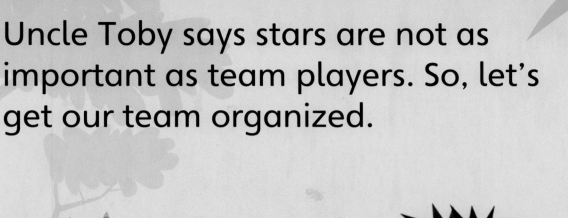

Uncle Toby says stars are not as important as team players. So, let's get our team organized.

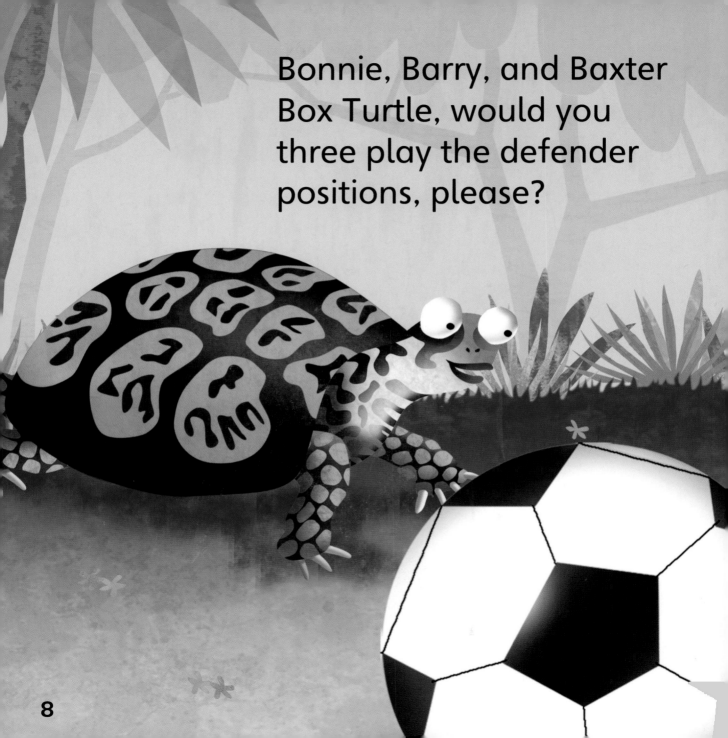

Bonnie, Barry, and Baxter Box Turtle, would you three play the defender positions, please?

8

9

We need five fantastic midfielders.

How about Harry and Helen Helmeted Turtle, Hermann Tortoise, and Sheri Spurred Tortoise joining me there?

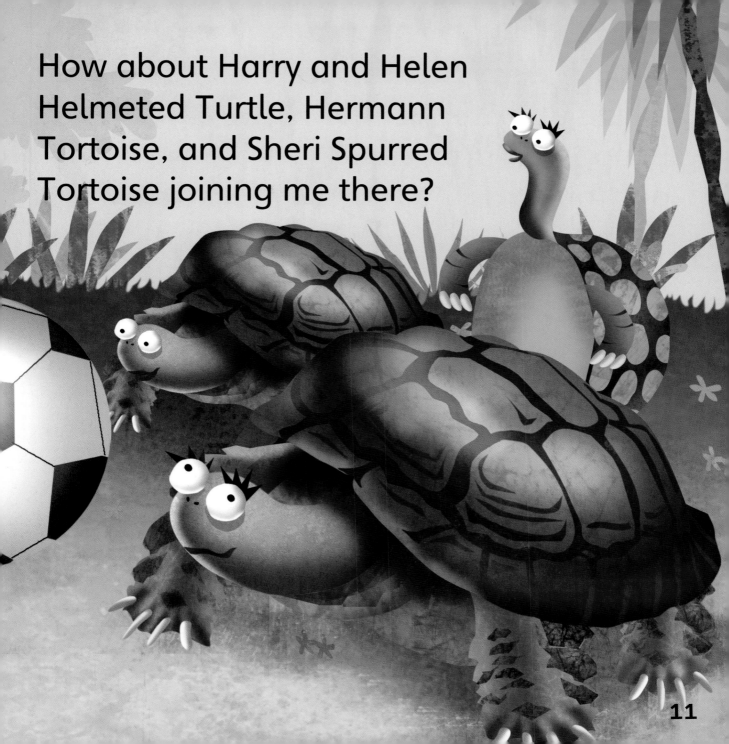

That leaves Patti Painted Turtle and Stephen Snapping Turtle for our forwards.

12

We all know they
are speedy and good
at kicking goals.

Of course, Gerry Giant Tortoise is our
excellent goalie.

Let's give him all the support we can.
Now, let the game begin.

15

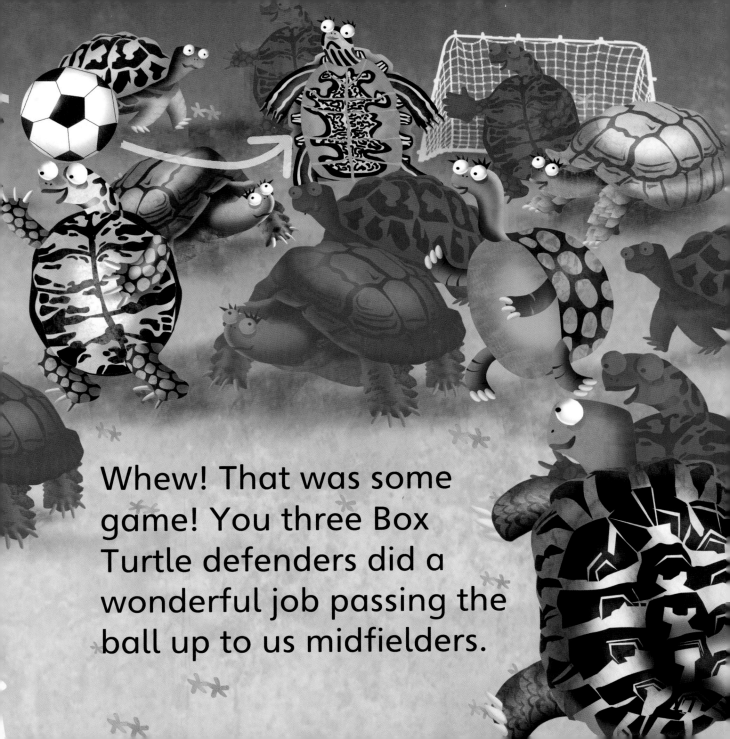

Whew! That was some game! You three Box Turtle defenders did a wonderful job passing the ball up to us midfielders.

Did you see how cleverly Hermann Tortoise shot the ball to Patti Painted Turtle? It caught the opposition off guard. Their goalie didn't even see it coming.

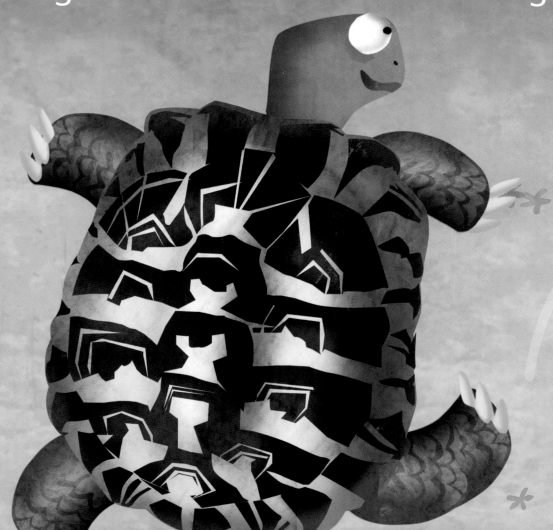

Our defensive crew assisted Gerry Giant Tortoise in keeping our opponents scoreless.

Let's hear it for our team captain, Tallulah Turtle, and the Tenacious Turtle's soccer team.

After Reading Activities

You and the Story...

Which team do you think won the game? Why?

What do you know about turtles that seems funny for them to play soccer?

Why do you think Tallulah mentioned her Uncle Toby?

How many players are on the Tenacious Turtle soccer team?

What position do you think you would play best on a soccer team?

Words You Know Now...

Choose from the words below and write four new sentences. Use one of the words in each sentence.

defender
defensive
goalie
midfielders
opponents

opposition
organized
tenacious
terrapin
tortoise

You Could...Help Your Friends Organize a Team

- Make a list of games.

- Research what equipment is needed for each game.

- Investigate places available for playing your game.

- Check on other teams playing in your area.

- Vote to choose the game and date you will play.

About the Author

J. Jean Robertson, also known as Bushka to her grandchildren and many other kids, lives in San Antonio, Florida with her husband. She is retired after many years of teaching. She loves to read, travel, write books for children, and watch her grandchildren play sports.

Ask The Author!
www.rem4students.com

About the Illustrator

Acclaimed for its versatility in style, Anita DuFalla's work has appeared in many educational books, newspaper articles, and business advertisements and on numerous posters, book and magazine covers, and even giftwraps. Anita's passion for pattern is evident in both her artwork and her collection of 400 patterned tights. She lives in the Friendship neighborhood of Pittsburgh, Pennsylvania with her son, Lucas.